To Seets, with love and gratitude.

And to my sweetie, Gregg.

Library of Congress Cataloging-in-Publication Data
Bramsen, Carin.
Hey, duck! / by Carin Bramsen.
p. cm.
Summary: A plucky duckling attempts to befriend a cat that just wants to be left alone.
ISBN 978-0-375-86990-7 (trade) — ISBN 978-0-375-96990-4 (lib. bdg.)
[1. Stories in rhyme. 2. Ducks—Fiction. 3. Animals—Infancy—Fiction. 4. Cats—Fiction. 5. Friendship—Fiction.] I. Title.
PZ8.3.B7324Hey 2013 [E]—dc23 2012001880
MANUFACTURED IN MALAYSIA
10 9 8 7 6 5 4 3 2 1   First Edition

Hey, Duck!

Carin Bramsen

Random House 🏠 New York

Hey, duck!

Why do you walk like that?

I slink because I am a cat.

Hey, duck!

Why is your tail so long?

Oh, please don't call me **duck.**
It's wrong.

Now leave me
so that I can sup.

Hey, duck!

Don't get your
feathers up.

**Such pretty
feathers,
by the way.**

Such pretty fur,
you mean to say.

Hey, duckie! Let's go play canoe,
and all the things that duck friends do.

We'll dance my favorite dance of all—
the **puddle stomp!**

We'll have a **ball!**

Oh, duck, why go off on your own?
We ducks can't stand to be alone.

Will you please note
that I'm a cat.
I want to be alone,
so
scat!

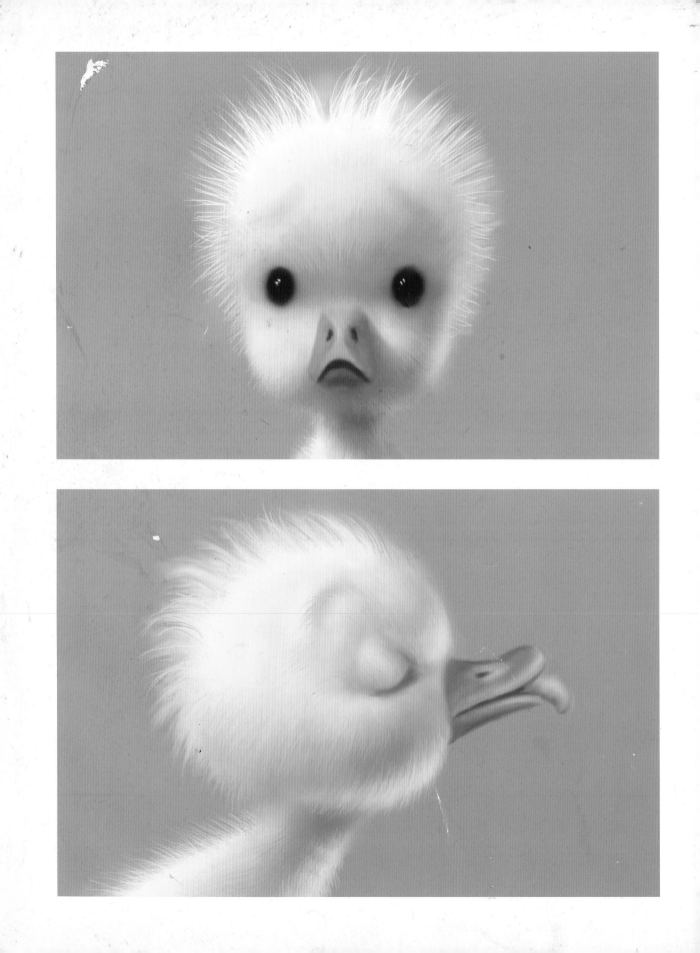

Who needs that
grumpy duck for fun?

I'll do the
puddle stomp
for one.

I have my own canoe to float.

That poor old duck has
missed the boat.

Missed the boat? Missed the boat . . .

MISSED THE BOAT!

Hello, my friend. You see I'm back.
And all I have to say is . . .

QUACK!

My sense of me has gone amuck!
I'm pretty sure I am a duck.
I'm not a cat, this much I know.
For no real cat would miss you so.

Oh, duckie dear! And I missed you!
Let's do the puddle stomp for **two!**

Uh-oh. Could I still be a cat?
I did not like that wet **kersplat.**

Well, duck or cat, you're my friend now,
which makes me want to shout . . .

MEOW!